The Mouse and the Princess:
Princess Eleanor's Curse

SIMON SIEN KANG

To order additional copies of this book, contact:
Xlibris
844-714-8691
www.Xlibris.com
Orders@Xlibris.com

ISBN: Softcover   978-1-6698-5867-6
        Hardcover   978-1-6698-5869-0
        EBook   978-1-6698-5868-3

Print information available on the last page

Rev. date: 01/24/2023

Hello there, dear reader. My name is Princess Eleanor. Ever since I was a baby, I was placed under a terrible curse by my evil uncle, Lord Balthazar. He turned me into a little mouse and wiped out my parents.

I began to lose all hope until one day I realized that I had a Fairy Godmother. She came to visit me and she gave me a potion that would turn me into a human by day, but still a cute little mouse at night.

Many years later, I saw a little brown mouse and a purple firefly wandering outside my castle window.

The little mouse entered my palace and I wanted to know who he and his little bug friend are. The little mouse said, "My name is Dredge and this is Beans and we only wish to seek shelter, Princess. Some wolves are after us."

I invited them to stay in my palace for as long as they liked and I welcomed them to my home.

Morning came up quickly and I was human again. My Fairy Godmother came to visit me and she turned me into a mouse as I didn't want Dredge and Beans to see me as a human yet.

"Why hello there." said my Fairy Godmother to Dredge. "I'm Eleanor's fairy godmother." "It's nice to meet you, Miss Fairy Godmother." said Dredge in a kind and sweet voice.

I told my Fairy Godmother that I was afraid to tell Dredge what my real form was like, but Fairy Godmother assured me that I'm beautiful no matter what form I'm in.

That night, a bunch of evil rats raided my room and mouse-napped me as they sacked me and threw me through some kind of magic portal. Rover tried to do his best to save me, but it was no use.

I realized that I was in the rat world and the Rat Prince was the ruler of it and he captured me as he wanted to marry me just so he could become king and rule over the domain as the Rat King.

I had to escape from the Rat Prince and his evil goons, so I ran away on all fours. I ran into Dredge who was sent by my Fairy Godmother to rescue me and together we ran into a deep hole.

We fell down the dark hole and we were in a world that was inhabited by mice who dressed just like humans did in my world.

The Rat Prince and his goons were closing in on us and just as we tried to fight back on our own, help arrived as a bunch of mice came to our rescue.

The kind mice, Evelyn and Ray and their children invited us into their home, which was shaped like the head of a mouse.

"Come have dinner with us." said Evelyn in a warm voice as she invited me and Dredge and to dine with them.

It was time to tell Dredge and the mouse family the truth. I told them I wasn't really a mouse. I was really a human princess trapped in the body of a mouse under a terrible curse which I hope can be reversed someday by a magic spell or true love's kiss. When they heard my tale, they were shocked and the mouse family and Dredge promised to help me find a way to break my awful curse.

That night, I had a dream. I saw my mother and father, the king and queen of Aris. They warned me that I should not be kissed by any mice especially Dredge since we had grown so close to each other or else I would be doomed to remain a mouse permanently and my curse would never be broken.

Morning came by so quickly and before I knew it, Evelyn called me and Dredge up.

Just as we were about to have breakfast, the Rat Prince and his evil goons were back and they invaded the mouse family's home and I felt something sharp on my body. I had been tranquilized!

I opened my eyes and I saw bars around me. "Eleanor, help!" cried out some squeaky voices. "Marry me, Eleanor and I will set all of you free." offered the evil Rat Prince. "Never!" I protested out to the filthy rat. "Then, I'll feed them to the Cat God." threatened the evil Rat Prince. I looked around at their desperate and scared faces. I told the Rat Prince I would marry him, but the Rat Prince decided to sacrifice Dredge as the Cat God needed at least one sacrifice. At least, that's what the Rat Prince told me.

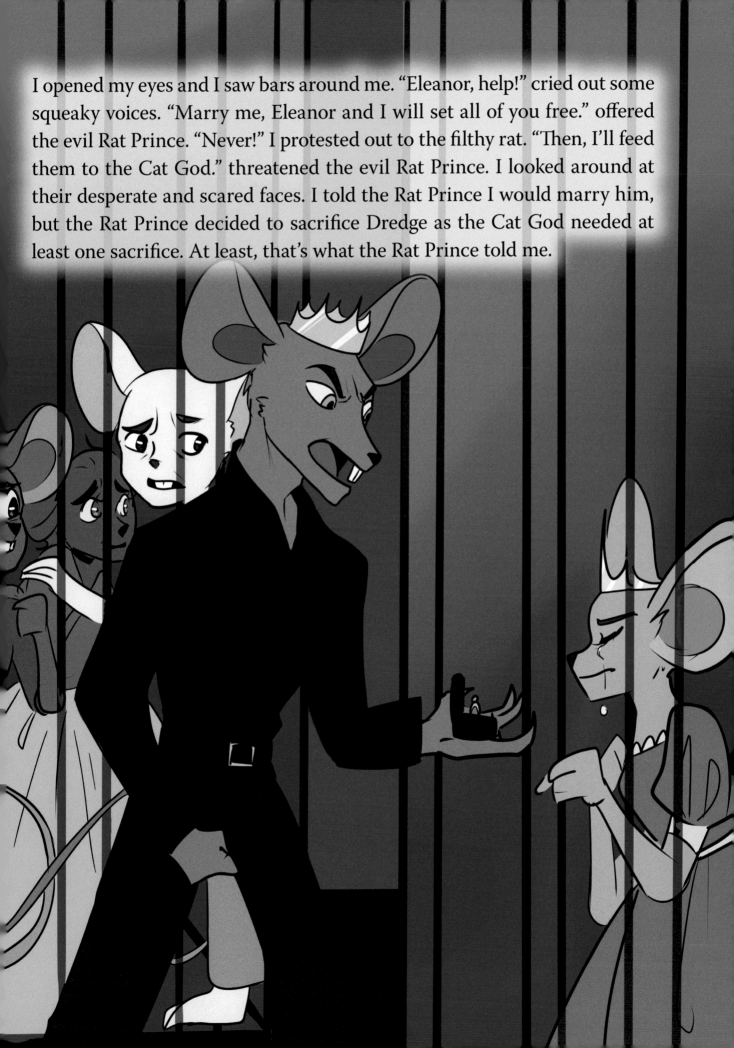

I was locked in a dark, filthy room all by myself and I began to cry. I didn't know what to do. I was all alone. I knew I had to find a way for me and Dredge to get out of this. There just has to be some way for us to outwit that evil rat.

Morning came very quickly and I was taken to the Rat Prince's throne to have my makeup done. The Rat Prince told me he wants me to stay as a mouse and live with him in the rat world forever.

A few hours later, we went to the ceremony.
I saw that Dredge was tied up by his tail.
ere was no cat seen to be a ywhere yet

Just as the Rat Prince began to introduce himself and the purpose of the ceremony, I stood up in a defiant manner and knocked the crown of the Rat Prince. I told the crowd that he was just an ordinary rat like everybody else. The Rat Prince grew angry and he tossed me into the ground where the Cat God awaits for his meal.

Just as I untied Dredge and freed him, the Cat God began to come after us. Fortunately, all of the rats and mice turned against the Rat Prince and they tossed him in the air and just as he was about to come after us, the Cat God snatched him in his jaws and swallowed him whole.

The Cat God was satisfied with his new sacrifice and he bowed at me and Dredge and left the grounds. All of the mice and rats formed a mouse ladder so we could climb up to safety.

Soon enough, a party was held for us and
Dredge and I began to dance.

As Dredge and I got closer to each other, he almost tried to kiss me and I pushed him away in a panicked move. I told Dredge that we couldn't be together anymore and in tears, Dredge left and ran away from me, heartbroken.

I ran off into the sewers and Evelyn tried to comfort me. I began to cry and my Fairy Godmother arrived and I asked her if she can transport me back to the human world, which she did. I said good-bye to the mouse family and I promised that we would meet again someday.

I was back in my bedroom and I was human again and I was reunited with my dear Rover once again. My Fairy Godmother arrived and Beans was alive and well too. She told me Dredge was in trouble as he was captured and adopted by my uncle, the evil Lord Balthazar at the orphanage.

I turned back into a little mouse again and I raced through the forest as my Fairy Godmother guided me to Lord Balthazar's evil lair. I was on a mission to save Dredge.

The moment we entered Lord Balthazar's evil lair, he trapped us in cages and when he revealed himself, he was nothing but a hideous rat just like the Rat Prince was back in the rat world.

Lord Balthazar wanted my blood and he told me we would both become human permanently, but boy, did that backfire. He pointed his amulet at me and I turned into a real mouse and Lord Balthazar became a man. He had transformed into a powerful sorcerer again.

Lord Balthazar cast a spell upon the entire kingdom and everyone began to turn into mice. "I shall rule over the kingdom with an iron fist. Everyone will obey me as I take my place as the new king of Aris!" proclaimed the evil sorcerer.

I had to find a way to save my kingdom and I saw that the amulet was controlling the horrible spell that was being cast upon the innocent citizens of Aris. I leaped at my evil uncle and after a few struggles, I ripped off the amulet with my teeth and it shattered to the ground into pieces!

"What have you done to me?" cried out my evil uncle. He had transformed back into a hideous rat again and he was about to lean in for the kill. But Dredge came to my rescue and he knocked over a bottle of rat poison into his mouth and Dredge and I kicked him in the face as he fell to his death from the tower of his evil lair.

I felt weak from my wounds and Dredge came over to me. I told Dredge that he could give me a kiss. Soon, a magical golden glow swarmed warmly over my body and I was trapped in the body of a mouse permanently. I wanted to care for Dredge more than anything in the world, so it was worth the decision that I made.

Another magical golden glow surrounded me and Dredge and when we opened our eyes, we were in the spirit world again. At first, my mother and father were disappointed that I wanted to stay a mouse, but they understood when I told them that I need to look after Dredge as he had no family left to look after him.

With a wave of her magic wand, my Fairy Godmother took us back to the human world and Dredge was officially my new son. Beans and Rover became our royal advisors and we lived in harmony together in the beautiful kingdom of Aris. All of the mice and rats from the mouse world lived peacefully in Aris as one and we all lived happily ever after. The End.

Printed in the United States
by Baker & Taylor Publisher Services